The Old Coot

The
Old Coot

by Peggy Christian
illustrated by Eileen Christelow

Atheneum   1991   New York

Collier Macmillan Canada
TORONTO

Maxwell Macmillan International Publishing Group
NEW YORK   OXFORD   SINGAPORE   SYDNEY

To Old Man Coyote (my father) who taught me
the power of story

—P.C.

Text copyright © 1991 by Peggy Christian
Illustrations copyright © 1991 by Eileen Christelow

Atheneum
Macmillan Publishing Company
866 Third Avenue
New York, NY 10022

Collier Macmillan Canada, Inc.
1200 Eglinton Avenue East
Suite 200
Don Mills, Ontario M3C 3N1

First edition
Printed in the United States of America
1   2   3   4   5   6   7   8   9   10
Designed by Kimberly M. Hauck

Library of Congress Cataloging-in-Publication Data

Christian, Peggy.
The old coot / by Peggy Christian.—1st ed.
p.   cm.
Summary: A prospector down on his luck is told wonderful
stories by a crafty coyote, and thereafter spends his life
retelling the stories around the Old West.
ISBN 0–689–31627–5
I. Title.
PZ7.C4528401   1991
[Fic]—dc20

Contents

1

The Old Coot and the Coyote

It was the townfolk that started calling him "the Old Coot." He'd come down from the hills twice yearly for supplies, and each time they saw him he appeared older and grubbier and more beaten down by life. The last few years had seen him cross that line between a tough old loner and a crazy man. Why, he'd gotten so antisocial, he'd as soon spit in your face as talk to you, and people said he was bad medicine.

But he wasn't always that way. When he'd first blowed into these parts, back in '84, he was just an eager young greenhorn fresh out of Iowa, come to the Black Hills to make him a fortune. Seems he'd been hankering after a gal back home, but her folks didn't cotton much to her marrying no poor dirt farmer. So he put out for the West to prove something to them, and swore he'd be back with a real bonanza.

Well, he got himself a grubstake and an ornery old mule whose owner sold him cheap, just to be shed of him. Then he set out for to find his big strike.

That first season went by and his luck was thinner than track soup. He barely had enough gold from panning to buy supplies. But he stocked up again, and headed back to the hills, despite it was coming on winter and most of the other prospectors was planning to shack up in town for the snowy season.

Well, that winter was a rough one, and though he survived it, it aged him some and still he'd found no gold. But he kept at it, year after year. The end of every season left him more and more bitter, and the harsh weather put more years on him than time had.

It was at the end of another summer, years later, that the Old Coot found out his gal had married someone else. But by then he didn't care. He'd pretty much forgotten she was the reason he was there in the first place, and anyhow, his mind was all eaten up with gold fever.

That fall, the first snow came before the trees had gotten a chance to shed their leaves, and it caught the Old Coot low on provisions with only one small nugget in his possibles sack. His situation seemed pretty desperate and he was feeling a mite despondent.

Then one night, as he was sitting by his fire eating one of his last cans of beans, he looked up and saw two specks of gold shining in the darkness. He thought for a minute they were gold nuggets, and he jumped up to reach for them, but they moved. He blinked his lids hard to see in the dark, and the fever cleared from his mind long enough for him to see that the nuggets were really the eyes of a coyote staring back at him.

"Evening, brother," the coyote said to him, as if it were a perfectly natural thing for a coyote to speak human.

Well, the Old Coot narrowed his eyes and started backing up towards where his shotgun was leaning against a tree. "You get now, you mangy varmint, or I'll blow you to kingdom come," he said.

"Easy," said the coyote. "I mean you no harm. I've come only to ask for a share of your supper and a place by your fire to sleep. It's getting pretty chilly at night and my winter coat isn't all grown in yet."

The Old Coot grabbed for the shotgun with his

hand. "Share my vittles, you say? Why, there isn't enough in the pot to feed a young boy, leastwise a grown man and a critter, too. Now you get or I'll be having coyote for dinner tomorrow."

He probably would have shot him on the spot, but he was a mite wary of a coyote that could talk.

"Surely you would not begrudge a fellow creature the warmth of a meal and some companionship?" the coyote asked. "Perhaps I could offer you something in trade?"

"What would a mangy old coyote have that I'd want? Like you said, your hide's not worth a plug nickel right now."

"Maybe not, but I do know where there is a river so rich the water runs gold. You could spend this lifetime and the next panning it and it would never run out," said the coyote.

The Old Coot's eyes lit up and the gold fever filled his brain. "If that be fact, and you're not tellin' a windy, then you best take me to it right now," he said, aiming the shotgun at the coyote.

"Put that gun away," said the coyote. "It would do you no good to shoot me, as you would never find the gold. And besides, it's dark out and I'm hungry, so let's just sit here and have our meal and a good night's rest, and in the morning I will start taking you to the gold."

"It best not be too far," the Old Coot said.

"Believe me, it's closer than you think. A few weeks' travel is all. But when you find it, you'll know it's been worth it."

So the Old Coot and Coyote ate the can of beans and then bedded down, but the Old Coot couldn't sleep a wink, his mind being all filled with visions of gold nuggets the size of horses' hooves.

The next morning Coyote set off a-whistling to himself and darting back and forth across the trail, inspecting things. And every so often he would trot along beside the Old Coot and start jawing with him, telling some tall tale or other. At first, the Old Coot didn't listen—still thinking about the gold, he was. But the trail was long and the mule reluctant—she not being too happy about traveling with a coyote and all. So the Old Coot began to give half an ear to the coyote's stories.

The first one he heard was so frightful it rose up all the hairs on the back of his neck and he was scared near plumb to death. He had to take a moment to remember where he was to get himself back together.

And then the coyote began a real tear-squeezer, and he told it in such a mournful way as to make water come to the Old Coot's eyes. The Old Coot shook his head and wiped the tears away with the back of his hand.

"I haven't cried in I don't know how long," he said, amazed at the feelings stirred up in his gullet.

But then the next tale was knce-slapping funny and the Old Coot burst out with a loud guffaw. "Darned if that don't feel good," he said. "My laughter's been a mite hard to find for the last few years."

That night, in the circle of the campfire, the Old Coot felt a bit more talkative, and he rested easier than he had before.

Well, the Old Coot and Coyote traveled on and on for weeks, the coyote providing an occasional rabbit to fill in for the dwindling supplies, and all the while he told stories—some frightful scary, some desperate sad, and some knee-slapping funny. At last they came to the edge of a wood, and it looked mighty familiar to the Old Coot. They started setting up camp, and the Old Coot pulled out the last can of beans from the pack bag.

"We're going to be in a heap of trouble if we don't find that gold soon," he said to the coyote. "This here's the last of the provisions."

"But you have found the gold already," the coyote said, with a mischievous look, and he flipped his tail at the Old Coot and trotted off into the forest.

"What in tarnation is that supposed to mean?" yelled the Old Coot after him. "You mangy, flea-bitten old prairie wolf! Come back here!"

But the coyote had disappeared. The Old Coot started to follow, but then remembered why the woods had seemed so familiar to him. Right over that hill yonder was the road to town. The old coyote had tricked him, leading him around in a big circle.

"Dad-gum coyotes! Tricksters and fools is all they are!" and he commenced cussing him out in his best United States English.

When his well of swear words had run dry, he gave up and sat down on a rock to reconnoiter. He was in a right bad fix now—not enough gold in his possibles sack to buy more than a week's worth of supplies, and game was mighty scarce this time of year. The only thing he could see to do was head down to town and ask if the storekeeper would grubstake him on credit.

The next day he lit out, and by late afternoon he was well on his way towards civilization. Just as the darkness started getting thick, he spied a cabin with a light glowing in its window. He went up to the door and knocked. A skinny young farmer with worry lines a-creasing up his face opened the door.

"What do you want, prospector?" he asked.

"Well, I'm feeling a mite gut-shrunk, and I was hoping you might have some vittles you could spare. I haven't got any gold to pay you with," he said, feeling real ashamed about asking for charity.

"No gold? And how's that?" the farmer asked him.

Well, you all just heard the story I recited to him, so I'll finish up by telling you that when my tale was through and the farmer had quit his laughing, he opened the door wide up, saying, "We haven't had anything around here for a long time to take the drudge out of the days. That story was just the thing. Worth more, I reckon, than a handful of gold. You know any more?"

And shore enough, I ended up staying there for a week, telling them folks all the stories Old Man Coyote had told me—some of them frightful scary, some desperate sad, and some knee-slapping funny.

Well, I've been drifting around ever since, stopping at one place or the other, and trading my pack of tales for a hot meal and a place to bed down. I've got me a real reputation now as a sagebrush philosopher, and folks are real hospitable wherever I go.

Late at night sometimes, when I hear the long, mournful howl of a coyote, I'll go and stand under the stars and howl right back to thank that mangy old trickster for the vein of gold he gave me.

2

The Old Coot
and the Rustler

I believe it was in '93 that this here scrape happened, and I reckon I can tell pretty near the truth about it, or as close as I can recollect. I'd been over in the Medicine Bow country, a-drifting from ranch to ranch with my pack-load of tales, and I'd been on the trail all day. It was getting nigh on to darkness when I saw the smoke of a campfire rising through the trees up ahead. Well, I struck out in that direction, thinking to find me some human companionship and maybe a bellyful of vittlcs.

When I reached the edge of the clearing, I peeked in to look the situation over, and when I got one good glance, I didn't have no call to take another. That wasn't any cooking fire, but a big old branding fire. And there was this feller, getting pretty handy with a running iron on a couple of calves. Changing the branded markings on them, he was, so he could steal them for his own. Well, it wasn't any of my concern, and I started to sneak on out of there, when my knob-headed old mule let out such a bellow as to wake the dead. That rustler turned around and seen me, and looked as surprised as a dog with his first porcupine. He grabbed his rifle and was on me quicker than a rattler.

"Bad luck, Old Coot," he says. "You alone?"

"Yep," says I. "Just me and this ornery old flea-bag. Passing through is all."

"Well, afraid you're just going to have to stay here for a spell. You see, I can't have you running off and letting them range riders know about my little op-eration here."

He snatched up a length of rope and shoved me over to a tree with his rifle muzzle. Then he com-menced to tie me up. Well, I didn't put up no resis-tance, figuring that kicking never gets you nowhere —unless you're a mule, of course. So he bound me to that tree tighter than a tick to a dog's back, and then went back to get my mule.

"You been rustling long?" I asked, by way of con-versation.

"Nope," he said, and I saw by looking him over he hadn't been too successful, because his boots were so frazzled he couldn't strike a match on them without burning his feet.

"Well, what are you planning to do with them, after they're yours?" I asked.

"I figure to start me a herd of my own," he said, "and this way's real quick and easy. Sure beats working!"

"Never heard of nobody drowning themselves in sweat," I said. "And what about the fellow you're stealing from?"

"Ah, he won't never miss them. He's got more than a man's entitled to, anyhow. I figure it this way: In a couple of years I'll be just as rich and important as him."

Well, he recommenced his work and I sat there for a spell watching that rustler messing with one calf and then the next. I got to considering what he might be planning for me when he'd finished the job. The possibilities conjured up by such a line of thought were real unsettling so I turned to less troublesome matters.

"How about a bit of fofarraw?" I asked. "I've got

me a pack-load of tales, and I'd be pleased to pull one out for you."

"I'm not interested in no Sunday school sermon," the rustler said. "What are you, anyhow—some kind of preacher man or something?"

"No. I'm no sin buster. Just a storyteller is all. I go around and trade my tales for a bite to eat or a place to bed down."

"Now there's an interesting line of work. And where did you get these tales of yours?"

"Oh, I get new ones everywhere I go. Someone's always telling me some tall tale or other, and I've got me a pretty good memory."

"Well, you tell me then, Old Coot: What's the difference between you stealing other people's stories and me stealing calves from that rancher fellow?"

"Well, you see, stories don't really belong to no one person," I told him. "Yarns and tales are a bit like wild horses, roaming around out there. When you hear one you like, you might try to rope it. But most times it gets away from you. Even if you manage to get a lasso around it, you still got to break it before you can get on and ride. And most likely it's going to have to be in your company for a spell until you

can really use it. Even then, it'll always belong to the wild. You'll never own it."

Well, by now that rustler had stopped messing with the calves and was setting down in front of me, rolling a smoke. I figured as long as I had his attention, I might as well try to be entertaining, so I commenced to tell him a story.

"All this has put me in mind of a tale I got from a Sioux over by the Crazy Mountains. It's about the crow and the hawk. See, one day this old crow, he was a-circling 'round above a snowy meadow, looking for something he could scavenge, when he looked up and saw old Hawk, a-soaring with the clouds across the sky. Well, Crow's heart got all filled up with envy and he thought to himself, 'If only I was as big and powerful as Hawk, I, too, could soar with the clouds.'

"Just then, Hawk swooped down past Crow and into the meadow, where he snatched up a rabbit in them big talons of his and flew away.

" 'Maybe if I were to eat what old Hawk eats, I could fly like him, too,' thought Crow, and he went right off to find Hawk.

"Soon as he spotted him a-setting there with his meal, Crow began a-squawking, making a raucous lot of commotion and signaling of danger. Hawk heard it and, leaving the rabbit in the snow, took off into the sky. Well, Crow flew right down and commenced eating on that rabbit. That stolen meat tasted mighty fine and Crow pecked away until every last bit was gone.

"Then he stretched out his wings to fly, but he couldn't get off the ground, being as stuffed as he was. 'A few more days,' he thought. 'Then I'll be soaring with the clouds like Hawk.'

"Well, this went on for a couple of more days—Crow following Hawk every time he made a catch and warning him off. Now Crow still wasn't able to fly any higher, but he was gittin' a lot plumper and that's a fact.

"Long about the fourth or fifth day, though, old Hawk got wise to him, and when Crow set up his squawking, Hawk just plain ignored him, and nothing Crow could do would get him to leave his catch.

"He kept following old Hawk, but every day, when Hawk caught something, he ate it all, leaving nothing for Crow to even peck at. Then one day, Hawk didn't come at all to the snowy meadow, and Crow started feeling kind of desperate. He was considering his plight when he saw a flash of movement below, and then he knew, sure as shooting, that if he wanted to eat, he'd have to do the hunting himself. He swooped down from that branch, kind of awkward at first, but as he closed in on the rabbit he felt stronger and surer than ever before. When he reached down and grasped at the fur, his claws were big and powerful like talons. And when he lifted off again, sure enough if the wing print he left in the snow wasn't that of a hawk."

When I'd finished my harangue, I looked over at the rustler, but he didn't say anything right off, and I decided to shut my trap and let him think on it for a spell.

After awhile he turned to me and said, "That was a right nice story, Old Coot, and I'd love to sit here and auger with you some more, but I've got me a lot of work to do tomorrow, so I best be getting some sleep."

Well, I guess I must have dozed off, too, although it wasn't the most comfortable I've ever been. Next morning when I woke, my hands were all untied, and there wasn't a sign of the rustler or the calves, except for the running iron on the ground by the cold fire.

Well, I got myself and my mule out of there real

quick-like, because being caught within a hundred miles of a running iron was a sure way to end up with a stiff rope around your neck and a short drop.

I never was too sure what happened to that rustler, but the next year when I stopped in at that particular ranch, the boss man told me the strangest thing had happened when they'd rounded up the cattle for market. A whole bunch of yearlings had big old scars over their brands, but there wasn't a one of them missing. I knew right then that there was probably one less rustler on this here Earth, and just maybe another hawk.

3

The Old Coot and the Gambling Man

It had been a month of Sundays since I'd been near any town, and having a pocketful of the long and needful green, I was feeling like I had the world by the tail with a downhill pull. So I blew into Virginia City with the first snowfall, bent on having me a real fandango.

Straightaway, I headed for the saloon and ordered up a bottle of the barkeep's finest whiskey, knowing I had a real educated thirst. I had just got my craw warmed up when I spotted a friendly game of cards a-going on in the corner. They looked to be short a player, and I offered to sit in a hand or two and try my luck.

But what I failed to notice right off was the un-natural size of one of the fellers' pile of winnings. It didn't take me overlong to figure out he was no cowhand, but a top-notch card sharp. Well, I decided what he needed was some distraction, so I figured to get him into an augering match and keep his mind from thinking of playing both ends against the middle.

I asked him what he did to make his way in the world and he didn't pull no punches. He told me right out.

"I'm a gambler, old man. A ways back I used to be a trapper, but the plews were getting scarce and I turned my talents to the cards. I figured it to be more profitable. After all, man's the only animal that can be skinned more than once."

Well, his words should've been sign enough to what was going to happen, but once a man has started gambling, it's hard for him to quit. I sat there playing hand after losing hand and watching more of my stake a-drifting over to the gambler's side of the table with each bet. In just a couple of hours, I'd lost every cent.

He asked me if there weren't nothing else I had of value, and I told him the only things left were my stories and my mule.

"Every man has a story or two, Old Coot, and

most of the time I can hear them for the price of a drink and a few minutes of time. What makes you think yours is worth more?"

"Well," I says, "I've got more than a few stories. So many, in fact, you'd be plumb tuckered before I ran out."

"Now there's a wager I'd be willing to make. Next to relieving greenhorns of their pay, my favorite thing is listening to stories. I've been searching out tales for nigh on to thirty years, and I'd like to see the man that could make me say 'Enough and no more.' "

Well, I figured maybe I had him on that one, and I said I'd be willing to make a wager that I was the one who could do it. He was sure enough interested, but wanted to see the mule before deciding the stakes.

We went outside and took a look at the old dragtail, and the gambler didn't seem none too impressed. But he agreed to make the bet and offered up his whole stack of winnings, so sure he was of victory.

Back inside, I commenced to tell him my stories. For forty nights we sat in that saloon, and I roped in one story after another, and still the gambler sat listening. By the end we'd attracted quite a crowd, and I was doing better than a patent medicine man.

But I went through my whole pack of tales—even taking a few spares out of my possibles sack—and I was running down faster than a two-dollar watch. But that old gamber just sat there enjoying every one.

"You know a lot of tales, Old Coot. But not enough to tire me out," he said, a-grinning with satisfaction. "Just to keep this interesting, though, I'll give you until tomorrow night to try to come up with something different."

Well, I don't normally draw to an inside straight, and I gave up prospecting some time back, but the sight of gold just laying 'round waiting to be picked up will always be a sore temptation. So I agreed, real sure I could find something before the next day.

I left the saloon and started walking down the street, sorting through all the tailings in my mind and looking for the show of color. But the more I studied on it, the muddier my mind was getting, and I was feeling a mite discouraged about the whole affair.

Then I heard a coyote a-howling in the woods outside of town. And I got to thinking, if I could just find that old trickster, he'd be certain to have some new tale I could tell.

Well, I traipsed through the snow into the woods, and sure enough if I didn't find his tracks a-leading off into the trees. I started following, but each time I thought I had him figured, his tracks would wander off in a new direction. It seemed to me he wasn't going anywhere and getting there pretty fast.

Well, I followed along until the tracks disappeared into a stream, but they didn't come out on the other side, and I had to wander up and down that stream for quite a spell before I spotted them again.

Then I was back on his trail, and it wound its way up to the top of this ridge. The going there got pretty tough, the rocks all slick from the snow, and I was having a fierce time getting a grip on them.

It occurred to me I might be getting sort of old for this kind of thing, but tracking down a good story is like hunting gold—once you get a hint of color, your mind just won't let go. So I pulled myself up over a couple of fallen trees, and there I was, up on top of a rocky ridge and not a track in sight. I looked all around me, but it was getting on to darkness, and the paleface moon wasn't shedding a whole lot of light on things.

I finally found his trail again, but darned if that

mangy old critter hadn't circled around and headed right back where he'd come from. I was feeling real disgusted: All that tracking had been about as useless as a four-card flush, and I hadn't found that old trickster, or a story, neither.

I headed back to the saloon trying to figure out what I would say, but my thinking was like a cow mired in a bog and sinking fast. I sat down at the gambler's table and ordered up a drink to scare away the cold. He eyed me real good, but I didn't let on that I was at a loss—still playing it real close to the chest, I was.

"Ante up, Old Coot," he said. "What have you been up to? You got a story for me or not?"

Well, I'm not one to be coyoting around the rim, but I figured I needed to stall for a little time, so I commenced to answer his first question and tell him about my day.

"After I left the saloon," I began, "I wandered off to the edge of town, and there I found a set of coyote tracks a-heading off into the woods."

I could plainly see at this point that the story was progressing mighty fast, and I'd best slow it down some to gain me more time.

"So these here tracks were heading off in a north-erly direction—or northwesterly, I guess you could say—but a bit more northerly than westerly, if you looked real close." I glanced at the gambler, and seeing the look on his face, I was as surprised as a nearsighted porcupine snuggling up to a cactus. He was getting impatient. Maybe I was on a roll.

"So anyways, this coyote, he took a step with his right front paw, and then a step with his left back paw, then a step with his left front paw, and then a step with his right back paw."

The gambler was squirming in his chair. "I get the picture, Old Coot. Then what happened?"

"Well, then he did it again—a step with his right front paw, then a step with his left back paw—"

The gambler leaned across the table toward me. "I got that part. Now get on with the story!"

"Well, then it was his left front paw, then the right back paw—"

"Just skip the details!" the gambler yelled, his face getting all red. "The story is the thing!"

"That's a fact," I says. "So then the coyote stepped with his right front paw, and then—"

"I know!" he screamed, slamming the table and

rattling his stack of winnings. "Just get on with it!"

"But a story's got to be told in its own way, in its own time. Besides, the story is about tracking the coyote and he left a lot of tracks. So the next one was with his left front paw—"

"Stop! I don't want to listen to any more of this!"

"And his next step was . . ."

"Enough, enough! You've won the bet, Old Coot!" And with that he scooped up all that gold and dumped it on the table in front of me.

Well, that old gambler walked out of the saloon, and nobody in that town ever seen his face again. I reckon that's about all you folks care to hear about it, and I'll just end up by saying that asking a man what he's been up to is the same as asking him how he feels: You rarely want the real answer. And the more I've pondered upon this statement, the more I am impressed with the probability of its truth.

4

The Old Coot
and the
Augering Match

Every once in a while there comes a time in a fellow's life when it seems like his luck has gotten stuck in quicksand and is sinking fast. Just when he thinks it's about to go under, though, he finds a rope lying around and manages to pull it out again. Now, that's just how things were last spring when I was roaming the range up near Cheyenne.

I still had my knob-headed old mule, of course, and the hundred dollars I'd won off that gambler was still in the mule's packs, so I was feeling pretty flush. Then it happened. We were traveling along nice and slow, and I suppose my mind was kind of drifting around like a tumbleweed, because one minute my mule was right behind me and the next minute he was plumb gone. I looked all around—and in that scrubby, flat country you can see quite a ways—but

there was no sign of him. And then I found it—
pretty near fell in it myself, as a matter of fact—a
hole in the ground. Must have been an abandoned
well or something. I peered down into it, but it was
as black as the inside of a cat. Then I tossed a rock
down and it was a full three minutes before I heard
it hit bottom, and I knew my mule and my grubstake
were goners.

For two days, I wanderd around in country as
empty as a cowboy's pocket after a night on the town,
until suddenly I spotted a lone rider on horseback
coming up over yonder ridge. I judged him to be
fairly peaceable, since he wasn't wearing no side iron,
and when he asked me my troubles I was glad to tell
him.

"I've gone and lost my mule," I said, "and every-
thing I had. As you can see, I'm in a desperate bad
way."

"Well, no you ain't," he said. "I'm an outrider for
a cattle outfit, and we've got a camp just on the other
side of that ridge."

"That's wonderous good, then," I said.

"Well, no it ain't. Our boss is so tight he wouldn't
give you the time of day for a dollar."

"But like I said, I haven't got nothing but the clothes on my back and a few tall tales in my head. This is desperate bad," I said.

"Well, no it ain't. He's also a great lover of tall tales and next to money, he likes tall-talking the best."

"That's wonderous good, then," I said.

"Well, no it ain't. We already got us a whole crew of truth stretchers, and tall tales run a dime a dozen in this outfit."

"That's desperate bad, then," I said.

"Well, no it ain't. As a matter of fact, we're having an augering match this very night, and the first one who can tell a story so tall that the boss calls him a liar will win claim to the finest roan mare in the remuda."

"That's wonderous good, then," I said, and waited for him to tell me otherwise—but this time he kept his mouth clamped shut and motioned for me to get on up behind him.

That night, after the grub was all eaten and the night crew had ridden out to watch over the herd, the rest of the outfit settled down for what promised to be a heap of hilarity. It don't take much to start a cowboy on a campaign against the truth, and you could tell by the chin-wagging going on that the augering match was about to begin.

A fellow named Gandy was the first one to take his chance at the roan, and he told a tale so tall your neck got sore from listening to it.

"I suppose you boys have all heard of Death Valley and know there's few men who have gone into it and come back to tell their story—but me and my young friend, Billy, are two such men.

"We were trying to get to California, back at the start of the gold rush, and we wanted to beat the other fellows out and get stake to a good claim. So, instead of traveling way around the desert like a man with any brains would have done, we decided to just cut across it.

"Now, Billy, he'd never seen a desert before, but I had me some experience with it, so I calculated how much grub and water we'd need and loaded it on a couple of mules. We traveled mostly at night, and we were but a couple of days shy of making the mountains, when danged if we didn't run into the worst luck. A fearsome sandstorm overtook us, and it was two days and two nights before it let up. When it was over, we found that our mules had up and disappeared and we were left out there in the middle of nowheres—and no food nor water, either.

"There wasn't nothing for it but to start walking and that's what we did. But after a few short hours we were plumb wore out. We'd already been two days without eating and the temperature in the shade was 130 degrees. But there wasn't any shade, so the temperature was more like 150. The sun can play some devilish tricks on you in heat like that, and we started seeing mirages—trees and lakes a shining off in the distance.

"Well, my partner, he'd never heard of mirages, and when he saw the lake, he got all excited and headed off to go fishing for some supper. I tried to tell him of his folly, but my tongue was too parched to move in my mouth, and I was too tired to follow, so I just lay down by a rock and fell asleep.

"When I woke up, I could smell fish frying, and sure enough, there was young Billy cooking up a mess of trout on the rock, it being as hot as a fry pan. He handed me his hat, and it was full of clean, cold water, and I took me a long swig, and then we commenced to make quick work of that fish dinner.

"When nothing was left but the bones, I laughed and told him it was the first time I'd ever eaten fish caught in a mirage, and then he asked me what a mirage was. Well, I told him those trees and lake we'd seen weren't really there—just a trick on our eyes from the sun—and he look real disappointed and said, 'You mean it was all a figment of my imagination?' and just as he said that, what was left of the bones disappeared, and the rest of the water dried right up out of his hat, and all I can say is, I sure am glad I waited until after we ate to tell him, because it gave us just enough energy to get the rest of the way across Death Valley."

When Gandy quit talking, every eye in the outfit turned to the boss to see what he'd make of this windy, but he just smiled and said, "That's a fine story, Gandy, and I believe every word, because if it weren't true, you'd have surely died on the desert and wouldn't have been here to tell it."

Well, it was apparent it would take a more vigorous stretching of the truth to win that mare, so the next fellow piped up with a tale even taller.

"Now I'm a hassayampa from way back and you fellows know that anyone who drinks from the Hassayampa Creek in Arizona can never again tell the truth. But this here tale I'm about to tell ought to have happened even if it never did.

"One day, a long time ago, before last winter or after this summer, I went out with some friends up the Yellowstone way to hunt jack-a-lopes. Now I suppose none of you fellows have ever heard of a jack-a-lope—and that's not surprising, as they're mighty rare—but as you all know, the Yellowstone country is full of oddities. So, to explain to you boys exactly what we was after, I'll tell you that a jack-a-lope has the body of a jackrabbit and the horns of an antelope. Catching one takes considerable skill and some real convoluted methods.

"We went out that night in the middle of the day, and traveled through a forest without a tree in sight. We came to the edge of a desert where the grass was so tall, you couldn't see over it, and sure enough, we spotted one of them jack-a-lopes drinking water out of a sand hill.

"I gave that critter the benefit of my most deliberate aim and fired my gun. Then I jumped up and caught the jack-a-lope just in time to grab my bullet out of the air and put it back in the chamber. I reached my arm down his mouth to skin him, and turned him inside out, and you may or may not believe it, but sure enough if I wasn't left with an antelope that had long fuzzy ears like a jackrabbit.

"The mystery of the thing is how those two critters ever got mixed up together in the first place, and I haven't got the slightest idea—but it's a fact and that's sure enough."

Now, I've heard some real circular stories before, but I was hard put to savvy such outlandish lingo, and I thought for certain that fellow had won. But the boss man just smiled.

"That's mighty farfetched," he allowed, "but I traveled with Jim Bridger for quite a spell, and he told me some wonderous things about that Yellowstone country—glass mountains, and water shooting up out of the ground higher than the trees. I was inclined at first to disbelieve him, but I found out later he hadn't mistold matters, and so I'm not going to cast any doubts on your story."

"If that whole thing ain't a lie, then nothing ever was," the outrider said. "Ain't nobody can top that one for pure fiddlefaddle."

Well, I figured that now might be a good time to

enter the match, the other fellow being so discouraged about their prospects. So I started off on a tale of my own.

"Now this here story ain't a story at all, but just a mere recitation of the facts as they happened to me. You see, I was down in town, not more than two whoops and a holler from here and I was riding the most beautiful roan mare, a lot like the one that you've got staked on this bet, in fact.

"Now, being as how I'd been out alone on the trail for quite a spell, I decided I needed some company and a little something to settle the dust, so I went into the closest eating house and had me some grub.

"When I came out a couple of hours later, what did I see but a fellow that looked just like you," I said, pointing to the boss of the outfit, "a-riding down the street on my horse. And I've been trying to catch up to him ever since!"

Well, one look at the boss's face and I feared I'd overplayed my hand. After all, accusing a man of horse stealing is inviting him to take a long drop on a short rope.

Then, all of a sudden, he started laughing and said, "You got me, Old Coot—caught me up in my own

loop with that one! If I call you the liar that you surely are, you'll win the bet, and if I don't, then I'm admitting the horse was yours all along—so you can take the mare, and anything else you might need."

So you see, folks, what looked to be a desperate bad situation actually turned out for the best. Not only was I finally shed of that dragtail old mule of mine, but I had me a mount that would make any man sit a little taller in the saddle.

Epilogue

Now, that old roan mare, she's served me well. But in spite of her good looks, she ain't got much character, and there's times when I been traveling for two or three days by my lonesome that I get to missing that ornery old mule of mine. I don't mind being lonesome, though; it gives me plenty of time to re-remember the stories I'm going to tell in a more interesting way. Now some folks might say that's stretching the blanket some, but I prefer to think of it as telling the stories the way they ought to have happened, and that way they're closer to the real truth than the actual facts are.

Just last week, in fact, when I was riding up near the head of the Big Muddy, I was working on taming a story I'd corralled at my last stop. Seems the feller there wasn't used to the big blows that can get going on the prairie, and he was telling me it got so windy he had to feed his chickens buckshot to keep 'em from blowing away.

Just as I said this part of the story out loud, a voice came out of nowhere and said, "Why, that's nothing. I've seen it blow so hard that a chicken setting into the wind laid the same egg five times."

I pricked up my ears and raised my eyes and searched the scrub all around, but I didn't catch sight of another feller anywheres. I was starting to pull my shotgun out of the scabbard real slow-like, when I caught sight of a flash of fur behind a serviceberry bush, and the next thing I knowed, I was looking into the face of Old Man Coyote hisself. He'd gone gray around the muzzle and looked a might grizzled, but I was plumb glad to see him.

That night we made camp together down by the river and spent the evening jawing in the firelight. I told story after story to the old chaparral fox—some frightful scary, some desperate sad, and some knee-slapping funny. But after a spell, I got to noticing Old Man Coyote was mighty quiet, especially for an old flannelmouth like him.

"What's the trouble, compadre?" I asked. He

looked as unhappy as a woodpecker in a petrified forest.

"Oh, it's good to hear the old tales again," he said. "It's good to see that someone still remembers them."

"Well, sure I remember," I said, and I got to reminiscing about the first time we'd met, when I was looking for gold in the Black Hills.

"Times are changing," the coyote said sadly. "The old days of crazy prospectors willing to share a meal with a sly coyote are gone. Now there's farmers and ranchers who think I'm a menace. They've got one thing on their minds and that's profit. They've killed off all the buffalo and their mangy cattle are riding roughshod over the range. The land and the stories—they don't mean anything to them."

His glumness was contagious, and I was starting to feel pretty low, for I had to admit the truth of what he was saying. It was getting mighty hard to find a place you could throw a rope without getting it caught on a fencepost. Howsomever, the situation didn't seem so desperate as he was making out.

"You know," I said, "that just makes the stories all that much more important. Once a feller knows the stories of a place, he's going to become a part of it. Hearing the stories sort of loosens the soil so a man can put down roots good and deep. The ones that won't listen—well, they're likely to blow away in the first good wind and keep up their wandering, like a tumbleweed."

"Now, that is true," said the coyote. "So you're more optimistic about the future?"

"Well, I don't know how optimistic I am, but I knows if we are going to have a chance against the speculators and land barons, then we got to work double hard to spread the stories, 'cause as long as the stories are kept breathing, the spirit of the place will stay alive."

The next morning, we parted company and I set off on my storytelling circuit with more eagerness than ever, determined to give mouth-to-mouth recitation to the spirit of the Old West.

Glossary

augering match: a talking contest

Big Muddy River: the Missouri River

chin wagging: social conversation

compadre: close friend, partner, companion

coyoting around the rim: talking all around a subject without getting to the point

fandango: a boisterous gathering, dance, or celebration

fiddlefaddle: nonsense

flannelmouth: someone who talks too much or a braggart

fofarraw: tall-tale telling

four card flush: a worthless hand (in poker, all five cards must be the same suit for the hand to be worth anything)

gold fever: a mania for seeking gold

57

grubstake: to furnish provisions with the understanding that profits will be shared

gut-shrunk: hungry

harangue: long-winded talking

hassayampa: a liar—someone incapable of telling the truth

long and needful green: money

outrider: a cowboy who rides around the range as a lookout

patent medicine man: a traveling salesman who peddled "miracle cures"—often nothing more than diluted whiskey

plews: beaver skins

possibles sack: a bag of dressed buffalo skin which held a trapper's personal belongings

remuda: the string of saddle horses on a cattle drive

running iron: a straight poker used as a branding iron to "write" whatever brand you wanted

sagebrush philosopher: a wise old storyteller

side iron: a pistol carried in a holster

tailings: the material left over after the ore has been extracted from the rock

telling a windy: telling a tall tale or a lie

track soup: soup made by melting animal tracks found in snow—that is, pure water

J   Christian, Peggy.
     The old coot. 104787

$11.9

J   Christian,
           Peggy.   104787

           The old coot.

$11.95

DATE	BORROWER'S NAME		